Dear Parents and Educators,

Welcome to Penguin Young Readers! As parents and educators, you know that each child develops at his or her own pace—in terms of speech, critical thinking, and, of course, reading. Penguin Young Readers recognizes this fact. As a result, each Penguin Young Readers book is assigned a traditional easy-to-read level (1–4) as well as a Guided Reading Level (A–P). Both of these systems will help you choose the right book for your child. Please refer to the back of each book for specific leveling information. Penguin Young Readers features esteemed authors and illustrators, stories about favorite characters, fascinating nonfiction, and more!

Max & Ruby: Max at School

LEVEL 2

GUIDED READING LEVEL **E**

This book is perfect for a **Progressing Reader** who:
- can figure out unknown words by using picture and context clues;
- can recognize beginning, middle, and ending sounds;
- can make and confirm predictions about what will happen in the text; and
- can distinguish between fiction and nonfiction.

Here are some **activities** you can do during and after reading this book:
- Make Predictions: At the end of this story, Max can't wait to go to school again. What do you think he will do at school the next day?
- Sight Words: Sight words are frequently used words that readers must know just by looking at them. They are known instantly, on sight. Knowing these words helps children develop into efficient readers. As you read the story, have the child point out the sight words below.

ask	how	thank	then	yellow
going	some	them	with	you

Remember, sharing the love of reading with a child is the best gift you can give!

—Sarah Fabiny, Editorial Director
    Penguin Young Readers program

*Penguin Young Readers are leveled by independent reviewers applying the standards developed by Irene Fountas and Gay Su Pinnell in *Matching Books to Readers: Using Leveled Books in Guided Reading*, Heinemann, 1999.

PENGUIN YOUNG READERS
An Imprint of Penguin Random House LLC

Penguin supports copyright. Copyright fuels creativity, encourages diverse voices,
promotes free speech, and creates a vibrant culture. Thank you for buying an authorized edition
of this book and for complying with copyright laws by not reproducing, scanning, or distributing any
part of it in any form without permission. You are supporting writers and allowing Penguin to
continue to publish books for every reader.

Cover art by Rosemary Wells.

Copyright © 2017 by Rosemary Wells. All rights reserved. Published by Penguin Young Readers,
an imprint of Penguin Random House LLC, 345 Hudson Street, New York, New York 10014.
Manufactured in China.

Library of Congress Cataloging-in-Publication Data is available.

ISBN 9780515157437 (pbk)   10 9 8 7 6 5 4 3 2 1
ISBN 9780515157444 (hc)   10 9 8 7 6 5 4 3 2 1

Max & Ruby!

Max at School

by Rosemary Wells
illustrated by Andrew Grey

Penguin Young Readers
An Imprint of Penguin Random House

Max gives Mama a kiss.

Ruby gives Papa a kiss.

"Bye-bye," say Mama and Papa.

"Bye-bye," say Ruby and Max.

Mama and Papa wave.

Ruby and Max wave.

They hop on the bus.

The big bus is yellow.

Max holds Ruby's hand.

Max is happy.

He has his book.

He has his lunch.

Max is going to school!

"Let's read our books,"

says Miss Bunty.

Max opens his book.

He looks at the pictures.

He tries to read the words.

Max can read the word CAT.

"Time to paint," says Miss Bunty.

Max uses blue paint.

Then Max uses red paint.

Max paints a truck.

"My truck is purple!" says Max.

"Time for lunch,"

says Miss Bunty.

Max opens his lunch box.

He has some juice, yogurt,

and an apple.

Max shares his apple with Lily.

Lily shares her cookie with Max.

"Time to play," says Miss Bunty.

José kicks the ball to Max.

Max kicks the ball hard.

"Goal!" says Max.

"Time for a nap,"

says Miss Bunty.

Max gets a mat.

Max gets a pillow.

Max closes his eyes.

Sweet dreams!

"Time for a song,"

says Miss Bunty.

Max sits on the floor.

Max, Lily, Vera, and José

sing the song.

They clap hands.

They tap feet.

"More songs!" says Max.

"Time for dress up,"

says Miss Bunty.

Max puts on a big hat.

Max puts on a big coat.

"I am a pirate!" says Max.

"Time to go home,"

says Miss Bunty.

Max gets his lunch box.

Max gets his book.

"Bye-bye, Miss Bunty," says Max.

"Thank you!"

Ruby meets Max.

They hop on the bus.

Max holds Ruby's hand.

The bus takes them home.

Max and Ruby wave.

Mama and Papa wave.

Max gives Mama a kiss.

Ruby gives Papa a kiss.

"How was school?"

ask Mama and Papa.

"School was fun!" says Max.

"Can I go back?"